DISCOVER SERIES
MAMMALS

Mamíferos

Búfalo Americano

American Buffalo

Oso Pardo

Brown Bear

Venado Macho

Buck

Alce Toro

Bull Elk

Caribú

Caribou

Coyote

Coyote

Gama

Doe

Bisonte Europeo

European Bison

Venado Hembra

Fawn

Zorro

Fox

Zorro Cachorro

Fox Cub

Toro Gelbvieh

Gelbvieh Bull

Alce

Moose

Cabra de Montaña

Mountain Goat

Mapache

Raccoon

Huskee Siberiano

Siberian Husky

Mofeta Rayada

Striped Skunk

Alce Sueco

Swedish Moose

Ciervo de Cola Blanca

Whitetail Deer

Jabalí

Wild Boar

Alce Amarillo

Yellow Elk

Hembra Joven

Young Doe

Make Sure to Check Out the Other Discover Series Books from Xist Publishing:

Published in the United States by Xist Publishing
www.xistpublishing.com
PO Box 61593 Irvine, CA 92602

© 2018 by Xist Publishing All rights reserved
Translated by Victor Santana
No portion of this book may be reproduced without express permission of the publisher
All images licensed from Fotolia
First Bilingual Edition

ISBN: 978-1-5324-0673-7   eISBN: 978-1-5324-0674-4

xist Publishing

www.ingramcontent.com/pod-product-compliance
Lightning Source LLC
LaVergne TN
LVHW070950070426
835507LV00030B/3486